S0-EIA-180

The Goosehill Gang

and the
Stitch-in-Time Solution

by Mary Blount Christian
illustrated by Betty Wind

I was naked and you clothed Me, I was sick and you visited Me,
I was in prison and you came to Me.
Matthew 25:36 RSV

Juv
C555
Sti

Publishing House
St. Louis

To Pat McKissack, with thanks

Concordia Publishing House, St. Louis, Missouri
Copyright © 1978 Concordia Publishing House
Manufactured in the United States of America

Library of Congress Cataloging in Publication Data

Christian, Mary Blount.
    The Goosehill gang and the stitch-in-time solution.

    SUMMARY: The "gang" helps Marcus' mother, an invalid, to be useful by involving
her talents in a Goosehill "clean-up compaign."
    [1. Physically handicapped—Fiction]
I. Wind, Betty. II. Title.
PZ7.C4528Gpr   [Fic]   78-702
ISBN 0-570-07357-X

Beth's breath made fog in the cold air as she spoke: "Hurry, Tubby! I'm freezing!"

Tubby took a couple of quick steps to catch up. "I hope whatever project we decide on will be an indoor one," he said.

Beth pulled her cap tighter. "I'm glad the teacher said we could work on our good citizen project together. That will be lots more fun."

Tubby nodded and unwrapped a piece of candy. He stuffed it into his mouth and threw the paper to the ground.

4

"Tubby!" Beth shouted.

"Mffft?" Tubby choked. "Good grief, Beth! You nearly scared me to death! What's the matter?"

"Oh, honestly!" Beth scolded. She pointed her gloved finger at the paper. "And we were just talking about good citizenship, too!"

Tubby grunted as he stooped to pick up the paper. "I don't see how my piece could make a difference. Just look around you."

Beth wrinkled her nose. "You're right! This is awful! It's like nobody cares anymore about Goosehill community."

Tubby nodded in agreement. "Hey, look!" he said. "There's Marcus!"

Beth waved to him. "Marcus! Wait for us!"

Marcus stood waiting. His shoulders drooped and his mouth was pinched.

"What's the matter, Marcus?" Tubby asked him.

7

"Aw," Marcus mumbled. "I just asked Mr. McGregor for a job at his store. And he said I was too little to work."

"Boy!" Tubby snapped. "Isn't that always the way? At home they tell us we are too big not to work!"

Beth stuffed her hands into her pockets and stamped her feet to keep warm. "Did you need the money for something special?"

Marcus shrugged. "Aw, I just wanted to buy my mom a gift. She seems so unhappy all the time."

Beth nodded. "Yeah, she's still in that old wheelchair. That's why!"

Tubby rolled his eyes. "Well, she can't change that! At least for a while, yet."

Beth knocked an icicle from the fence as she passed by. "I know that. But you know how awful you feel when you're too sick to play and too well to stay in bed?"

The boys nodded sympathetically. Marcus said, "There's Pete and Don on my front steps." They joined the others and the five of them went inside.

Mrs. Moreno greeted them. "I put some hot chocolate on the stove. But I couldn't reach the cups, of course."

Marcus pulled the cups from the cabinet and poured the chocolate. "Now for the surprise," he said. He pulled off his jacket. The others gathered around staring at his t-shirt.

"Hey!" Pete said. "A real Goosehill Gang t-shirt!"

"Where'd you get that?" Tubby shouted.

For once Beth didn't say anything.

Marcus grinned and nodded toward his mother. "She embroidered over that rip I got going over the fence."

Mrs. Moreno nodded. "I'll make each of you one if you get the thread and the shirt," she said.

"Wow!" Beth said. "Real Goosehill Gang t-shirts. Now we'll really look like a club!"

The gang settled around the kitchen table. Beth fingered the scraps of material lying before her. "I didn't know you were so talented!" Beth exclaimed.

Mrs. Moreno laughed. "I used to work at a dress shop before I got so sick. I personalized things for the customers."

Pete cleared his throat. "We'd better get the Goosehill Gang meeting started. First we want to thank Mrs. Moreno for letting us meet here. It's too cold in the treehouse."

16

He tapped the side of his cup. "Now. Do you
have any ideas about what we can do for our good
citizen project?"

Don spoke. "Why don't we make posters? You
know, something catchy like:
    BE A GOLDEN EGG.
    KEEP GOOSEHILL CLEAN."

Tubby nodded enthusiastically.

"Humpft!" Beth snorted. "Some citizens need more than a poster!"

Tubby slumped back, blushing.

Don nodded. "Yeah I was noticing on the way over that papers and junk were scattered everwhere."

"Even the litter cans are so dingy you can't recognize them anymore," Pete added.

Beth began to fidget. "Why don't we choose two or three blocks and clean them up?"

"Oh, my aching muscles!" Tubby moaned. "What happened to that neat idea about posters?"

Beth ignored Tubby. "Mrs. Moreno, how soon could you do our t-shirts?"

"Why, right away! I have nothing else to do."

Beth grinned. "Then we'd look real official. We could visit store owners and get them to donate paint and brushes and plants and stuff."

Tubby moaned. "Paint? Brushes? Plants?" Beth flashed a look at him. "Anybody can do posters. But the Goosehill Gang is special! We should do something special too!"

They decided to paint the bus stop benches and put plants wherever they could.

"We'll probably have to print a sign saying, "Donated by so and so," Pete said.

"Is there anything I can do?" Mrs. Moreno asked.

Suddenly Beth jumped out of her chair. "Yes! Oh, yes, there is!"

Everyone waited for Beth to speak. "I was thinking about Don's idea about golden eggs. Could you embroider some kind of egg patch that people could wear?"

Mrs. Moreno laughed. "Of course! That will be fun!"

The next few days Mrs. Moreno embroidered t-shirts and egg patches.

"She smiles so much!" Marcus reported. "It's like magic!"

Beth nodded knowingly. "I told you so. She needed to feel useful."

With their t-shirts on, the Goosehill Gang visited the mayor's office. They gave him a patch to wear.

The mayor called in newspaper and television reporters. He smiled a lot and showed them his

patch. "We need more good news about children," he told them.

The entire gang was on the six o'clock news that evening. Store owners began calling to donate everything they needed for the project.

Every day after school the children worked. Beth and Don painted benches. Tubby planted rose bushes around the bandstand in the town square.

Marcus painted the litter cans. And Pete printed on
each can:
    MAKE LITTER JUST
    A DROP IN THE BUCKET.

Don, Pete, Tubby, and Beth met at the tree house after school. "I didn't see a single can or piece of paper on the street today," Don reported. "I think people are really going to take care of Goosehill now."

Tubby pulled the last rose thorn from his

blistered hands. "I hope so. I really do. I wouldn't want to do this again!"

Beth laughed and shoved her paint-stained hands in front of him. "Look at me! I'm from Mars!"

Marcus hurried up the ladder. "Mom is so excited. But she won't tell me a thing unless all of you are there, too."

When they arrived, Mrs. Moreno's eyes sparkled at them. "Wonderful news!" she said. "The mayor's wife came here today. They want me to design and make a community flag! Can you imagine?"

Beth clapped her hands. "Why you are a modern Betsy Ross!"

"There's more!" Mrs. Moreno said. "She has promised to help me start my own little business right here! I can sew right here!"

Marcus jumped up and gave his mom a hug. The others crowded around her chattering at once.

"We'll help!" Beth shouted. "We can fix you a room right here. And we can pick up and deliver your orders and . . . ."

Tubby rolled back moaning. "Please! This time, let's do posters!"